Rue, The Monster of Insecurity

The Nose That Didn't Fit

a WorryWoo tale

by Andi Green

ISBN 978-0-9792860-1-8
Manufactured in China

First edition, 2008
Second edition, 2009

To see all The WorryWoo Monsters™
go to www.WorryWoos.com

This book is dedicated to my Dad.
Thanks for telling me to keep pounding my
heart and never give up.

the fact

that his

nose was a

very **large** size.

He thought that his snout just didn't fit...

and wished everyday it would shrink quite a bit.

When he saw his reflection

he'd frown at the sight.

"How to Look Better"

he'd read through the night.

From nose caps

to new tricks

Rue tried to pretend,

that his nose was the same as that of his friends.

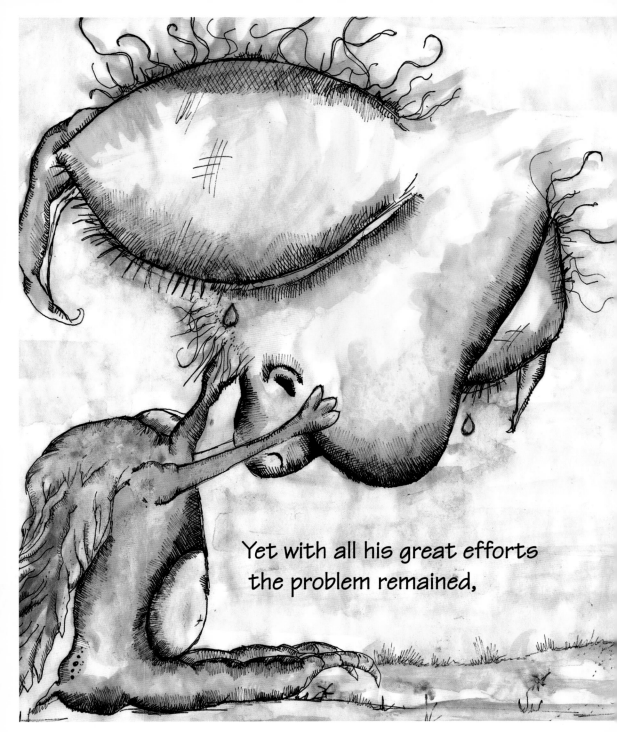

Yet with all his great efforts
the problem remained,

he had a **big** nose and

he wanted it changed.

"Oh what should I do," Rue said to himself.

"I must find **The Wizard** and ask for his help!"

So, he searched and he searched,
feeling hopeless until...

...he found
the great wizard
on top of a hill.

"Oh Magic One,"

Rue began to implore,

"The way that I look I can't stand anymore!"

"Others
have noses
that fit them so
snuggly, but I
have this honker
that makes
me feel **ugly.**"

"Oh, it isn't your nose,"

The Wizard said with a grumble

Confused by these words, Rue let out a

GRUNT...

And said with a pout,

"I know
what
I want!"

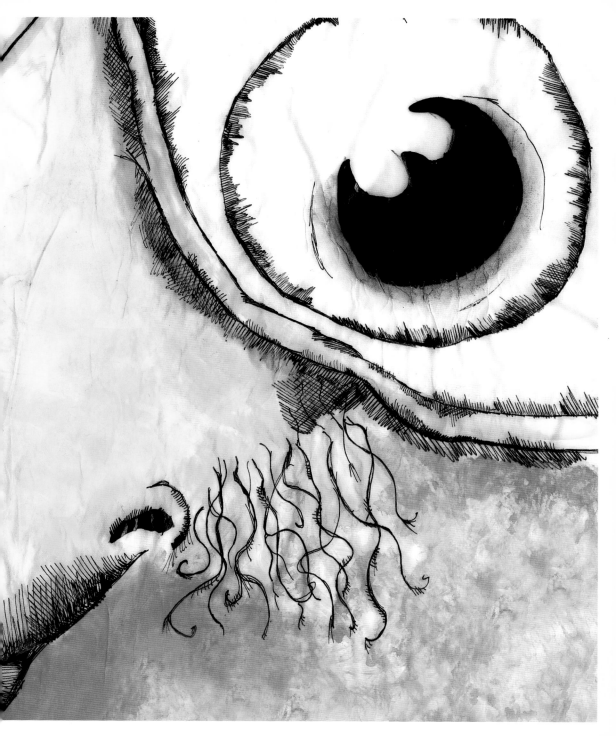

Nodding his head, The Wizard turned

...and just for one second it rained lima beans.

With a whirl

and a poof

and a puff

and a

WEEEEEEE...

Rue's nose
was shrunk to
the size of a
pea!

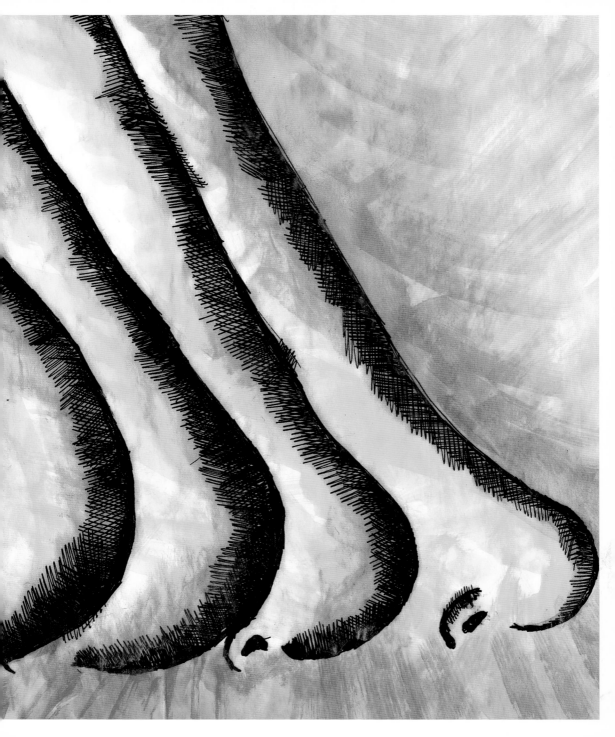

Jumping for joy

he went on his way,
not hearing the last words
The Wizard did say...

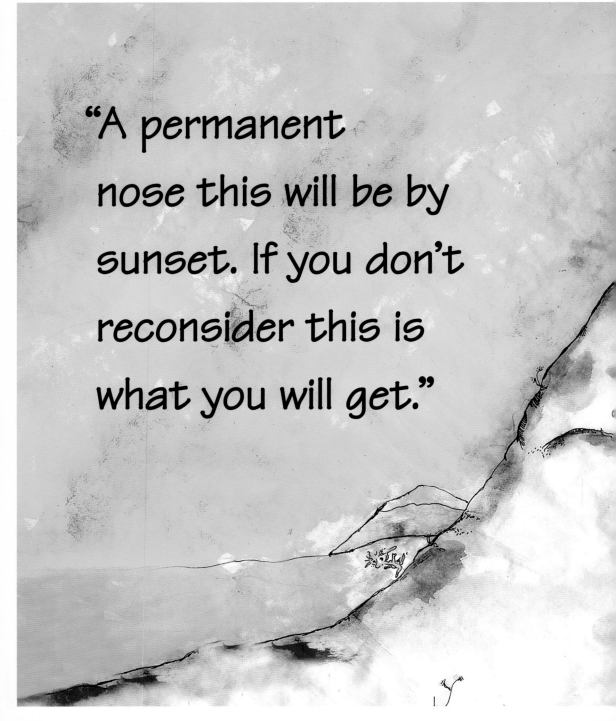

"A permanent nose this will be by sunset. If you don't reconsider this is what you will get."

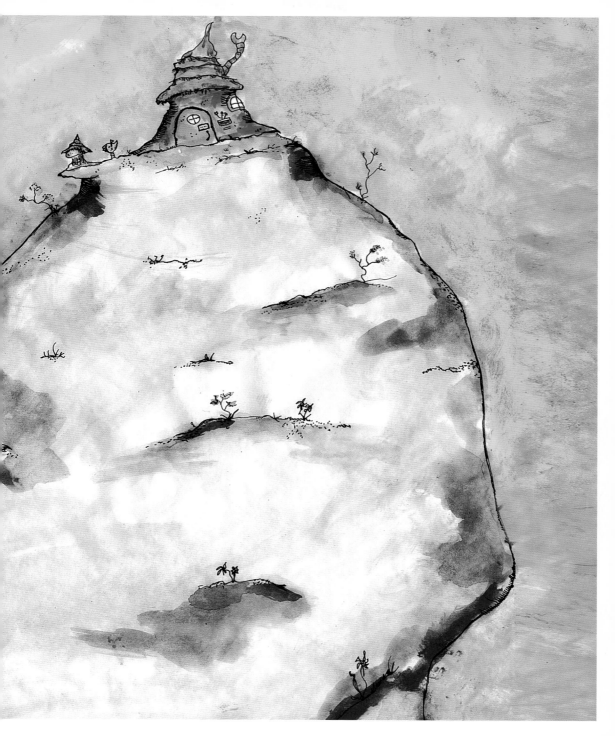

At the bottom of the hill Rue pranced all about,
hoping that someone
would notice his snout.

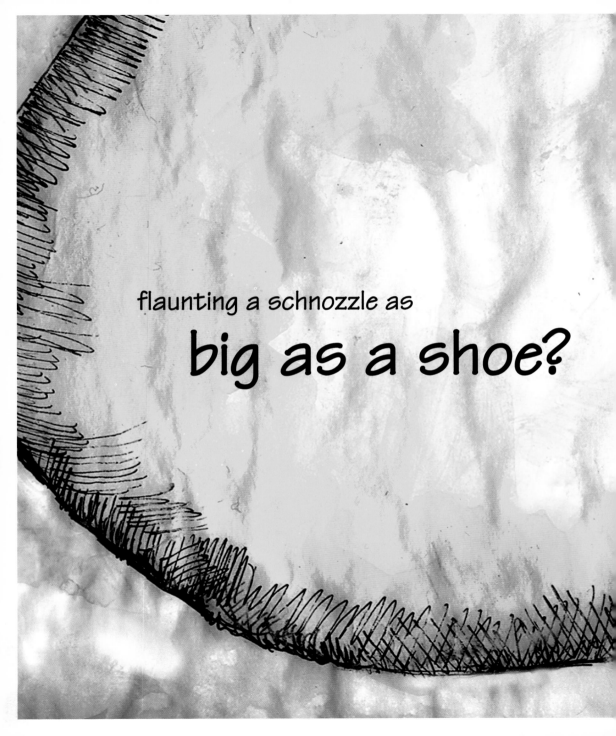

flaunting a schnozzle as

big as a shoe?

A monster so **lovely**

Rue was awed by her grace,

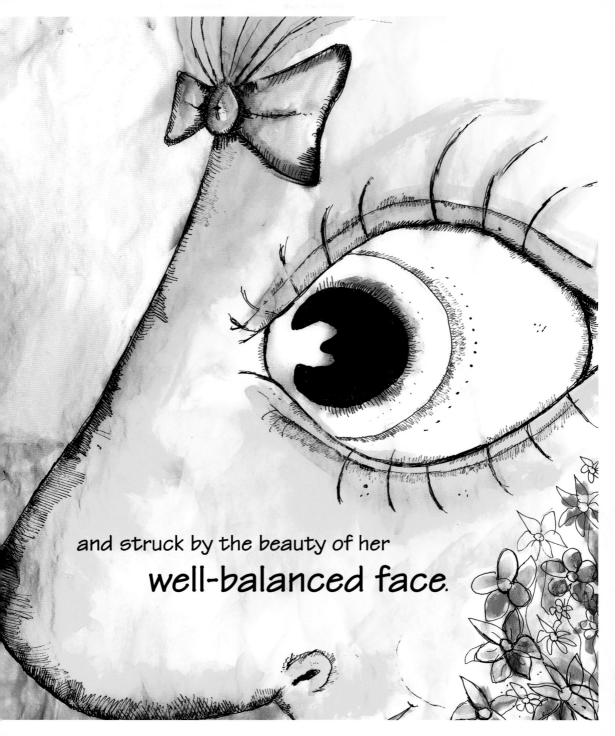

and struck by the beauty of her
well-balanced face.

"Pardon me sir,

I've been looking all night,

for the one they call Rue but he's nowhere in sight."

"I hear that he's **funny** and **sweet** and so **kind,**

and the best part of all is his

nose is like mine!"

"I thought you were HE but I see that's not true,

you have such a **small** nose,
you couldn't be Rue!"

Crushed by her words,

Rue felt very sad, for he wished he could show her the nose he once had.

A nose just like hers that had **fit** him so well,

the same one that changed with the lima bean spell.

"What have I done," he whispered in wonder,
"I think I've committed a horrible blunder!"

As he uttered these words
the sky turned bright green.

And

what

fell

on

his

head...

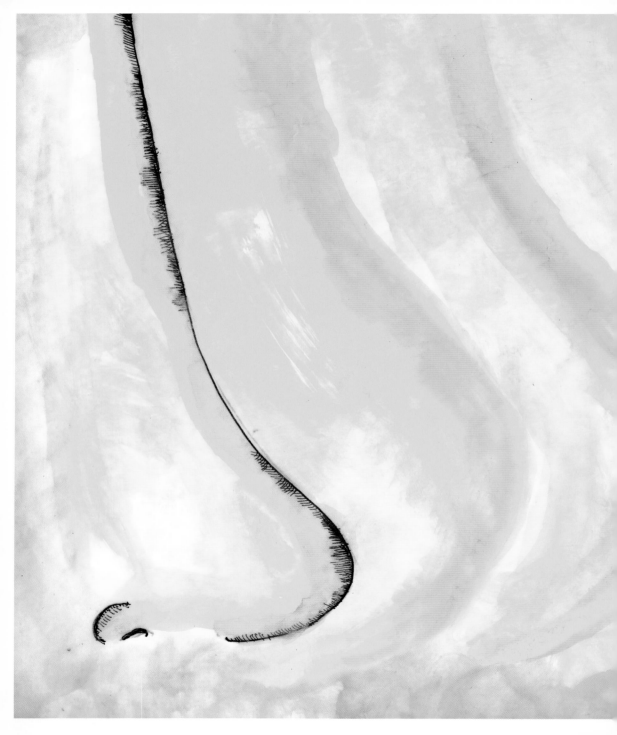

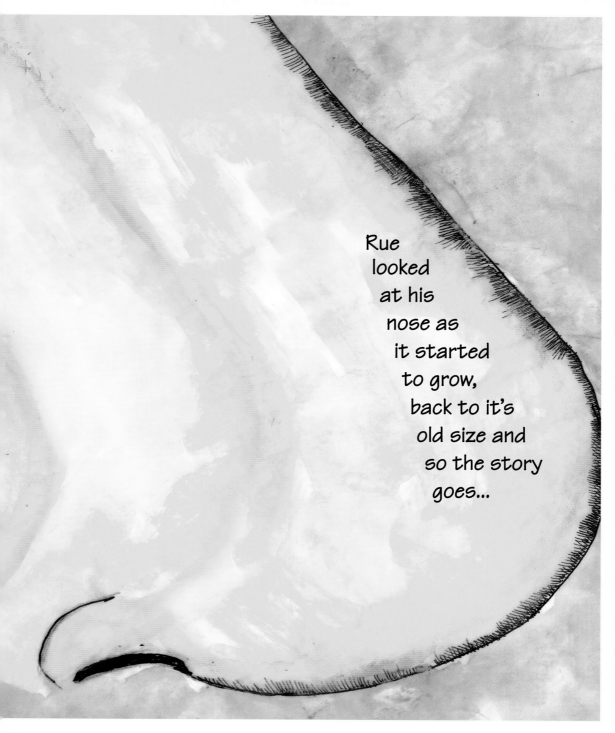

Rue
looked
at his
nose as
it started
to grow,
back to it's
old size and
so the story
goes...

He heard in the clouds the wizard from afar,

"Be true to yourself and love who you are."

And after that day Rue never did hide...

the fact that his nose was a very large size.

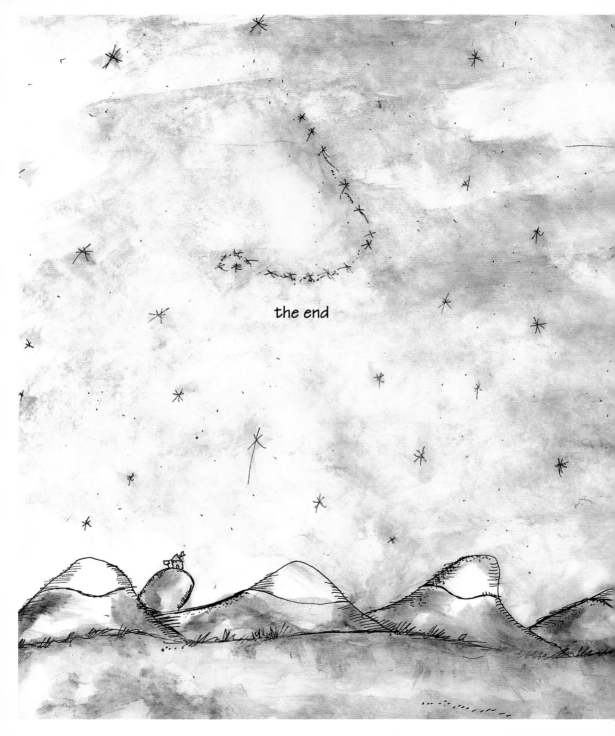

the end

www.WorryWoos.com